THE USBORNE
ANIMAL
QUIZBOOK

Paul Dowswell

Edited by Judy Tatchell

Designed by Ruth Russell

Illustrated by Ian Jackson and Rachel Lockwood

Additional illustrations by Chris Lyon and John Shackell

Consultant: Gillian Standring

Contents

About this book

There are over two million different kinds of animal in the world. Even baking deserts, the frozen poles, and the deepest oceans have their own unique inhabitants. This book looks at how animals behave, and how they cope with the different environments in which they live.

How to do the quizzes

Throughout the book, there are quiz questions to answer as you go along, printed in italic type, *like this.* Some of the questions rely on your general knowledge, others have clues elsewhere on the page. Keep a note of your answers and check them against the answers on page 28-31.

The Megaquiz

On pages 26-27 is the Megaquiz – a set of ten quick quizzes to test you on what you have read about in the book. You can check your answers on page 32.

The animal world

There are an extraordinary number of different sizes, shapes and colours in the animal world. These two pages look at the main types of animals and how they fit into their environment.

Scientists have divided the animal world into various groups. Animals in the same group, or class, have similar features, and behave in similar ways. A particular kind of animal, such as a lion or an ostrich, is known as a species. Some of the main groups are shown here.

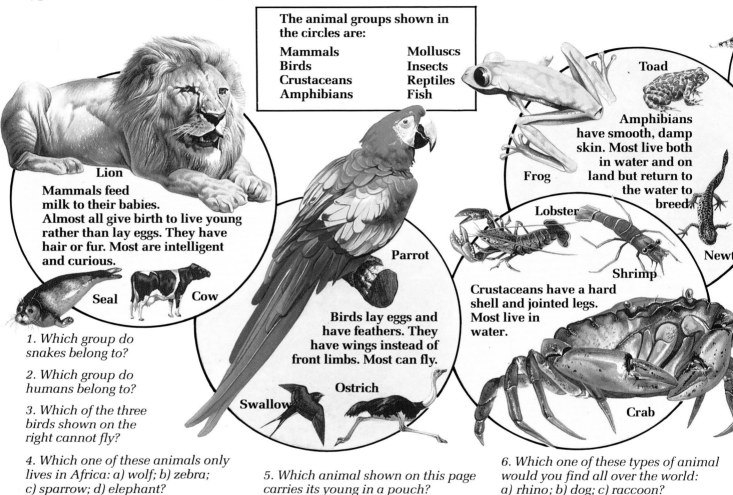

The animal groups shown in the circles are:

Mammals
Birds
Crustaceans
Amphibians

Molluscs
Insects
Reptiles
Fish

Lion

Mammals feed milk to their babies. Almost all give birth to live young rather than lay eggs. They have hair or fur. Most are intelligent and curious.

Seal

Cow

Parrot

Birds lay eggs and have feathers. They have wings instead of front limbs. Most can fly.

Ostrich

Swallow

Toad

Amphibians have smooth, damp skin. Most live both in water and on land but return to the water to breed.

Frog

Newt

Lobster

Shrimp

Crustaceans have a hard shell and jointed legs. Most live in water.

Crab

1. Which group do snakes belong to?

2. Which group do humans belong to?

3. Which of the three birds shown on the right cannot fly?

4. Which one of these animals only lives in Africa: a) wolf; b) zebra; c) sparrow; d) elephant?

5. Which animal shown on this page carries its young in a pouch?

6. Which one of these types of animal would you find all over the world: a) rhino; b) dog; c) raccoon?

Why are some animals only found in certain parts of the world?

Many animals, such as sparrows, beetles and rats, are found in every continent. They can fly, or have been carried on boats. They all eat a variety of foods, and can cope with different climates. Other animals are only found in certain areas. Here are three reasons why.

The three-toed sloth eats cecropia tree leaves, found in South American forests.

The polar bear's thick fur coat suits a cold environment.

The kangaroos of Australia could live elsewhere. The ocean between Australia and the rest of the world prevents them from travelling.

1. They only eat food found in the area they live in.

2. They can only live within a certain range of temperatures.

3. They cannot travel long distances because of barriers like oceans or mountains.

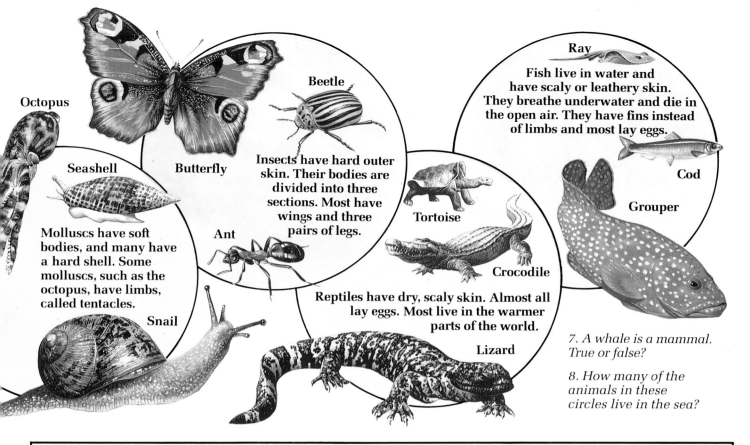

Octopus

Seashell

Butterfly

Ant

Molluscs have soft bodies, and many have a hard shell. Some molluscs, such as the octopus, have limbs, called tentacles.

Snail

Beetle

Insects have hard outer skin. Their bodies are divided into three sections. Most have wings and three pairs of legs.

Tortoise

Crocodile

Reptiles have dry, scaly skin. Almost all lay eggs. Most live in the warmer parts of the world.

Lizard

Ray

Fish live in water and have scaly or leathery skin. They breathe underwater and die in the open air. They have fins instead of limbs and most lay eggs.

Cod

Grouper

7. A whale is a mammal. True or false?

8. How many of the animals in these circles live in the sea?

How do animals fit into their environment?

Animal species can change their appearance and behaviour to fit their environment. This can take thousands of years, and is called evolution. Here you can see how two different sorts of fish have evolved to fit into two completely different kinds of environment.

Tall, narrow bodies help angelfish shelter in coral reefs.

Muscular bodies help barracuda swim huge distances in the ocean.

9. Which one of these is a fish: a) starfish; b) dolphin; c) salmon?

10. Which scientist first suggested the theory of evolution: a) Charles Darwin; b) Galileo; c) Isaac Newton?

Did you know?

Three-quarters of all known animal species are insects. A third of all known insect species are beetles.

11. Which one of these is not an insect: a) moth; b) termite; c) iguana; d) locust?

What are food chains?

All animals need to eat plants or other animals to give them energy to survive. Plant-eating animals, called herbivores, are eaten by meat-eating animals (carnivores). These may be eaten in turn by other carnivores. This sequence is called a food chain. Within the chain, energy from food passes from one living thing to another. An animal that hunts another animal is called a predator. The animal that is hunted is called prey.

Here is a simple food chain, showing who eats who.

Domestic cat

Blue tit

Greenfly

Plant

12. Is a lion a carnivore or a herbivore?

13. When one kind of animal dies out this is called: a) extinction; b) exhaustion; c) exhibitionism.

14. The Ancient Egyptians worshipped cats. True or false?

15. Can you put this food chain in the right order? thrush caterpillar fox cabbage

Animal families

Apart from staying alive, producing the next generation is an animal's strongest instinct. These two pages look at how animals care for their young.

How many babies do animals have?

The number of eggs or babies that an animal has depends on the type of animal. The giant clam makes millions of eggs every year. Most are eaten by other animals but a few may survive. The sperm whale, though, only has one baby every three or four years.

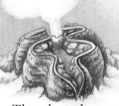

The clam releases millions of eggs into the water around it.

The clam does nothing to look after its offspring. The whale, on the other hand, provides its calf with milk for at least two years.

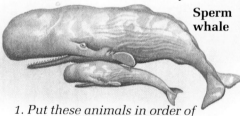

Sperm whale

1. Put these animals in order of size: a) elephant; b) sperm whale; c) giant clam.

How do penguins hatch their eggs?

In order to hatch, birds' eggs need warmth. In Antarctica, the male emperor penguin warms an egg by perching it on its feet under a fold of skin. This keeps it away from the frozen ground. The penguin stays still over the egg for eight weeks waiting for it to hatch.

Emperor penguin

Once hatched, the chick stays next to the warmth of the parent's body.

2. Warming an egg to hatch it is called: a) incineration; b) invitation; c) incubation.

Young penguins too big to shelter under their parents, huddle together to keep warm.

3. What do penguins eat?

4. Penguins fly north for the winter. True or false?

Why do baby animals look different from adults?

Some young animals have different body coverings from the parents. Ducklings, for example, are covered with soft, brown feathers called down. Down keeps them warm and is good camouflage. As they get older, they grow stiffer feathers which help them to fly.

5. Which is bigger, a duck's egg or a hen's egg?

A young emperor angelfish looks very different from an adult. This is to stop an adult mistaking it for a rival for food and mates, and fighting it.

6. Which one of these is not a real fish: a) angelfish; b) butterflyfish; c) flying fish; d) rocket fish?

How does a young gorilla learn gorilla manners?

Gorillas live in large groups. While they are growing up they learn how to get on with their group. They become adults when they are between seven and ten years old.

This young gorilla is practising its grooming skills, removing dirt and insects from the other gorilla's fur.

The baby learns by watching everything the mother does.

Pretend fights show who is stronger and who to treat with respect.

8. Are gorillas carnivores or herbivores?

7. Gorillas beat their chests: a) to make themselves cough; b) to look threatening; c) to crush fleas.

How do animals shelter their young?

Some animals build a nest or den for their young to keep them safe. Many birds, for instance, build nests high up in trees, or on cliff ledges.

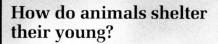

9. Which bird lays its egg in another bird's nest?

Polar bears build a den under the snow for their cubs.

Entrance tunnel ← Ventilation hole

Kangaroos carry their young in a pouch – a sort of built-in nest.

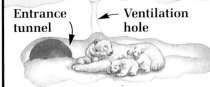

10. Kangaroos are only found in one continent. Which one?

Did you know?

The female praying mantis eats her mate. This provides her with energy to lay eggs.

Where does a crocodile lay its eggs?

Crocodiles lay their eggs in a nest of plants near the river bank and cover them with mud. The mother stands guard over them. The baby crocodiles make squeaking noises to let the mother know they have hatched. She breaks into the nest, and takes them in her mouth to the river, where they are safer from predators.

11. Crocodiles cover their eggs with mud: a) to hide them; b) to keep them warm; c) to stop them breaking.

12. A Korean circus once taught a couple of crocodiles to waltz. True or false?

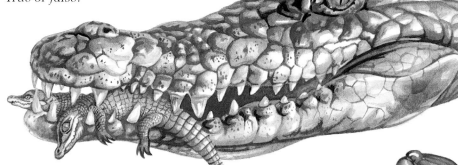

Why might a scorpion eat her young?

Scorpions are very aggressive meat-eaters. If they are hungry they may even eat their young. They can produce another large brood very easily.

Scorpions carry their young on their backs.

13. Baby scorpions sometimes eat each other. True or false?

Are queen bees different from other bees?

Although thousands of bees live together, only one bee, called a queen, lays eggs. Male bees, called drones, mate with the queen. Female bees, called workers, look after the eggs.

14. Honeybees show other bees where to find food by: a) dancing; b) singing; c) buzzing.

15. What are these cells made of?

The queen bee lays eggs in these cells.

Queen

Worker

Staying alive

These two pages look at how some animals hunt, and how other animals avoid being eaten.

What makes a good hunter?

The Indian tiger, like all tigers, has the abilities a good hunter needs. It has speed, strength, sharp senses and a talent for moving silently. Its skills and senses enable it to catch all kinds of animals, from young elephants to birds. Many of its features are found in other meat-eating animals.

Camouflage stripes make the tiger almost invisible in long grass.

Over short distances, the tiger can run as fast as antelope and deer, its swiftest prey.

1. Tigers can hide in grass as short as 60cm (2ft). True or false?

2. The tiger's favourite food is: a) wild pig; b) potatoes; c) people.

The body is flexible enough to run, pounce and crawl. The tiger can climb trees to catch birds and monkeys.

Good hearing, sight and smell help find prey.

The strong jaw can kill in a single bite.

Sharp claws come out when the tiger attacks.

Why do some animals hunt in packs?

Some animals, such as wolves, hunt in packs because it enables them to attack prey bigger and stronger than themselves. They are also likely to catch more food. They have to share their catch with the rest of the pack.

Other animals, such as leopards, hunt alone. They only attack smaller or weaker prey. However, when they do catch anything they do not have to share it with other animals.

3. Where do leopards usually hide their prey after they have killed it?

4. Which of these animals is the wolf's nearest animal relative: a) tiger; b) rat; c) poodle?

5. Which one of these animals hunts in a pack: a) harpy eagle; b) lion; c) giant anteater?

How do animals hunt their prey?

Hunters who are not especially strong or fast have to use special tricks to get close enough to their prey to catch them. Here are some examples.

Some animals, such as moray eels, hide themselves and lie in wait for their prey.

Moray eel

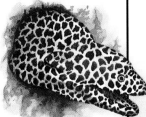

6. A moray eel can grow to:
a) 1m (3.3ft);
b) 3m (10ft);
c) 30m (100ft).

Some animals, like this heron, use bait to attract prey.

The heron waves a feather which a fish might mistake for a fly.

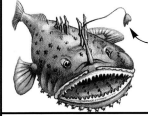

7. What do you think the angler fish does with this?

Animals that move slower than their prey might use a trap. Many spiders weave a sticky web to catch insects.

8. Spiders eat their webs. True or false?

Some animals have their own weapons. The chameleon has a sticky tongue curled up inside its mouth which shoots out to capture insects.

9. The chameleon can change colour to suit its surroundings. True or false?

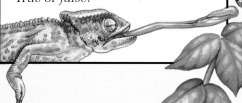

How do animals protect themselves?

Animals only fight to defend themselves as a last resort. Here are some of the ways in which animals try to escape from predators.

Camouflage colouring helps an animal blend in with its environment. Some animals, like the sole, can even change colour to match their surroundings.

10. If a sole is placed on a chess board it will match the squares. True or false?

Some animals try to trick an attacker into thinking they are more dangerous than they really are.

Cats fluff up their fur to look bigger.

The Io moth has a pattern like a frightening face on its wings.

Animals that sting, such as bees and wasps, inject poison into an enemy.

11. Bees die if they sting. True or false?

Some animals offer a part of themselves to eat. They hope this will distract an attacker, and also satisfy its appetite.

12. Which of these animals can break off a part of itself: a) parrot; b) lizard; c) donkey?

If starfish are attacked they can shed an arm. A new one will grow.

How do animals avoid attack?

The size and strength of large animals like elephants make them difficult to kill. Most smaller animals avoid danger by hiding or running away. Healthy animals are seldom caught. It is usually the old, very young, sick or injured who are eaten. They are too slow to escape.

Like many plant-eaters, deer gather in herds. They are safer in groups than on their own.

New-born deer can walk almost immediately. This helps them stay with their herd.

13. What are baby deer called?

Over long distances, the deer can outrun most attackers. The feet can be used to kick if the deer is cornered.

14. Which one of these is not a type of deer: a) caribou; b) elk; c) llama?

How can bright colours protect an animal?

Some small animals, such as this cinnabar caterpillar, have bright colours to warn hunters that they are poisonous and taste horrible.

15. What do caterpillars turn into?

Spotted deer are good at defending themselves. They have certain features, found in many plant-eating animals, which help them escape from hunters.

Antlers can jab an attacker.

Good sight and hearing alert the deer to danger.

Male spotted deer

The long neck gives a good view of the surroundings.

Female spotted deer

Spotted camouflage helps hide the deer in grass and forest.

Did you know?

Some crabs defend themselves by placing sea anemones, which have stinging tentacles, on their claws.

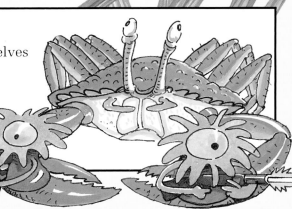

Northern forest animals

Much of the land in the far north of the world is covered with forest. These forests, shown in white on the map, almost circle the Earth.

The forest provides animals with a shield from harsh Arctic winds, and a good supply of food – at least in the warmer months. Compared with other parts of the world, though, there are few animals here, especially in the winter.

1. Which three continents contain northern forests?

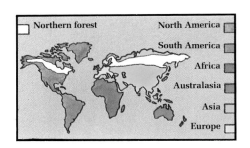

Northern forest	North America
	South America
	Africa
	Australasia
	Asia
	Europe

How do animals survive the winter?

In the winter the forest is covered with snow and the temperature can drop to −40°C (−40°F). There is little to eat and it is difficult for the animals of the forest to keep themselves warm.

Lynx

In the winter a lynx may have to hunt over an area of 200 square kilometres (80 square miles) to find enough food to stay alive.

2. Why have humans hunted the lynx in the past?

3. Which one of the animals on this page is named after a type of tree found in the northern forest?

Moose

The moose eats as much as it can in the summer. It stores this food as fat on its body, for the harsh winter months.

4. The moose is a type of deer. True or false?

Many of the smaller mammals, like this woodchuck, save their energy by hibernating (sleeping through the winter months).

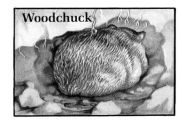

Woodchuck

To survive without eating, the woodchuck slows its heartbeat from 80 beats a minute to four. Breathing drops from 28 breaths a minute to one.

Pine marten

The pine marten, like most northern forest mammals, has a thick fur coat to keep it warm.

5. Which of these is not a good spot to hibernate in: a) underground; b) hollow tree; c) cave; d) tree top?

What is the forest like in the spring and summer?

Spring brings great changes. Snow melts, trees and flowers bloom, and insect eggs hatch. Lemmings, voles and other small animals come out of hibernation and breed in great numbers.

When summer arrives the forest is like an overflowing larder. There is so much food that birds such as the wood warbler migrate from further south to spend the summer here.

Wood warbler

6. Which one of these animals migrates: a) python; b) thrush; c) dormouse; d) oyster?

7. Which one of these animals is the lemming's greatest enemy: a) owl; b) vole; c) wood warbler?

Lemming

Why do beavers build dams?

Beavers are found throughout the northern forests. They protect themselves from predators by building a large nest called a lodge and flooding the area around it. They do this by building a dam on a stream.

8. In which one of these countries would you find beavers: a) Chile; b) Italy; c) Canada?

9. Beavers build small canals to ferry logs to their dams. True or false?

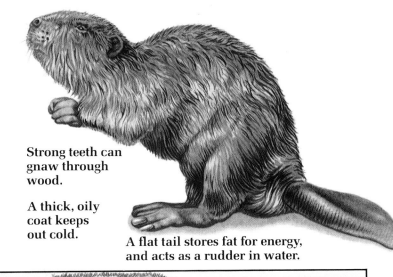

Strong teeth can gnaw through wood.

A thick, oily coat keeps out cold.

A flat tail stores fat for energy, and acts as a rudder in water.

The dam is made of wood, grass and mud. It keeps the entrance to the lodge underwater.

10. What do you think the lodge is made of?

11. Why is the entrance underwater?

A male and female beaver live here with their family.

How do bears bring up their cubs?

Bear cubs stay with their mother for two years. She protects them fiercely and teaches them what to eat. Bears are not normally friendly with each other, but bear mothers sometimes babysit for other bears. They may even adopt another mother bear's cubs if the mother dies.

Bears stand up to get a better view of their surroundings.

Bear cubs learn hunting skills by watching their mother.

12. Bears build igloos to shelter in during the winter. True or false?

13. These bears are: a) koala bears; b) grizzly bears; c) Himalayan bears; d) polar bears.

14. Which one of these games have humans taught bears to play: a) ice hockey; b) hopscotch; c) Scrabble?

15. A bear can eat 200,000 berries in a single day. True or false?

Bears love to eat salmon, which they catch with their paws.

Did you know?

In the forests of northern Japan, volcanic springs form pools full of hot water. Macaque monkeys can keep themselves warm in the cold winter by soaking in these pools.

Why is it dangerous to feed bears?

Bears love the food humans eat. Once they have tasted it they may venture into campsites and towns looking for more. Many bears that do this are shot as they can be dangerous.

Rainforest animals

Because most rainforests are hot and damp, the trees and plants that grow in them are the biggest in the world. These forests provide so much food and shelter that far more animals live here than in most other environments.

Most of the animals shown here come from South America, which has the largest single forest in the world. Rainforests are shown in white on the map.

1. Which continent on this map does not have a rainforest?

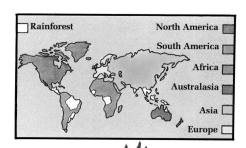

Rainforest | North America
South America
Africa
Australasia
Asia
Europe

What do rainforests look like?

Rainforests have four main layers.

At the top are the tallest trees, called "emergents".

The tops of other trees form a roof, or "canopy", to the forest.

Beneath the canopy is another layer of trees.

The final layer is the forest floor.

Who lives at the top?

Birds and the lightest, most agile climbers live at the top of the forest. Harpy eagles live here. They eat other birds and small mammals. Many animals stay away from this level to avoid them.

2. This harpy eagle could carry off a monkey. True or false?

Are sloths really lazy?

Sloths do everything very slowly. The leaves they eat take a long time to digest and convert into energy, so they need to save their strength. They sleep often and hang motionless for hours when awake.

Sloths come down from the trees once a week to excrete. This is when they are most likely to be attacked and eaten.

3. Jaguars find sleeping sloths by listening for them snoring. True or false?

4. How many hours a day do sloths sleep: a) 3; b) 15 to 18; c) over 24?

Strong claws grip the branches.

Tiny green plants called algae grow over their fur. This helps to camouflage them. Moths often live in the fur.

The fur grows from stomach to back. This lets rain drip off easily.

Who lives at the bottom?

Animals that cannot fly or climb live on the forest floor. Capybaras, tapirs and millions of insects live here.

Jaguars hide in low branches and drop on their prey. They eat tapirs and other plant-eaters.

5. Jaguars don't hunt at the top of trees because they are afraid of: a) heights; b) harpy eagles; c) breaking thinner branches.

The capybara is over 1m (3ft) long. Capybaras are rodents, like rats and squirrels.

The tapir is a shy plant-eater which only comes out at night. It picks up food with its trunk.

6. The capybara is the largest rodent in the world. True or false?

7. A tapir only comes out at night because it eats bats. True or false?

How are animals suited to life in the trees?

Most animals that live in the forest can either fly or climb.

The spider monkey has a flexible tail which can grasp branches.

The parrot's short, broad wings help it fly through the gaps between trees and branches.

8. What sort of food do parrots eat?

9. Which is not a type of parrot: a) cockatoo; b) parakeet; c) macaw; d) condor?

The marmoset, like all climbers, has long paws to help it grip.

10. Which two rainforest animals on these two pages is the marmoset most similar to?

11. A marmoset is about the size of a kitten. True or false?

How can animals fly without wings?

Some rainforest animals in Africa and Asia have body shapes which help them glide between trees.

Gliding snakes flatten their bodies in flight.

Flying frogs have large webbed feet for gliding.

Flying squirrels have large skin flaps.

Did you know?

The arrow-poison frog is so venomous that some South American tribes dip arrows into the poison to make them more deadly. A frog 2.5cm (1in) long makes poison for 50 arrows.

How big is an army of army ants?

When army ants go out looking for food, up to 200,000 of them march in a column 20m (66ft) wide. They move at about 14m (46ft) per hour capturing spiders, cockroaches, scorpions and ants.

12. Do army ants move quicker than a sloth?

13. Do people live in the rainforest?

Why is the rainforest so noisy?

Many rainforest animals claim an area for themselves. They make a lot of noise to warn others to keep away from their territory.

Howler monkeys make an eerie howling noise every morning and evening.

14. The sound of a howler monkey's howl travels: a) 1km (0.6 miles); b) 5km (3 miles); c) 16km (10 miles).

15. Which one is the quietest: a) spider monkey; b) tapir; c) parrot?

City wildlife

Ever since towns and cities were first built 8,000 years ago, wild animals have lived in them. The city provides two things that all animals need: plenty of food and shelter.

What sort of animals live in the city?

City animals need to be tough enough to stand noise, pollution and bustle. They have to be able to live close to people and eat a variety of foods. They need to breed easily and make use of all kinds of available space for shelter.

City dustbins provide food for foxes.

Rats and mice live wherever food is stored or left out. Rats can live almost anywhere, even in sewers, but mice prefer warmer places. Rats are tough and can eat many kinds of food, including meat. They can breed at an alarming rate.

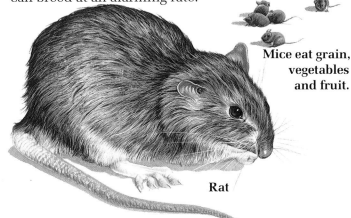

Mice eat grain, vegetables and fruit.

Rat

Bats live in caves in the wild. Attics and towers provide similar shelter in cities.

Pigeon

Pigeons have evolved from seashore birds that nest in cliffs. They feel at home sheltering in the nooks and crannies of tall buildings.

1. Which one of the animals on this page did the legendary Pied Piper drive out of the town of Hamelin?

Insects like silverfish, houseflies and cockroaches compete with each other for food and shelter.

House fly

2. Which one of these is not a real insect: a) clothes moth; b) tile termite; c) furniture beetle?

3. How long does a fly live: a) ten hours; b) ten days; c) ten weeks?

4. Mice grow up to be rats. True or false?

5. A female rat can have twelve babies every: a) twenty minutes; b) eight weeks; c) two years.

6. Which animal shown on this page is seen the most in cities?

Did you know?

Termites that live in the city will eat anything – even plastic-coated wiring which has no food value at all. Nobody knows why they do this.

Why don't more animals live in the city?

Many animals are unsuited to the food and shelter the city provides.

Here are some of the reasons why not all animals can live in the city.

An animal such as the hippopotamus would be too large to find shelter in the city. Foxes are usually the biggest city animals. 	**Some animals cannot find the food that they need in a city. Pandas, for example, can only eat bamboo, which they find in the forests of western China.** 	**Some animals, such as deer, are too timid to live in the crowded, noisy city.** 
Animals large and fierce enough to attack and eat humans, like this tiger, would be killed if they came into a city to look for food. 	**Some animals cannot live with the noise, smoke, fumes and dirty water of the city. This butterflyfish needs clean, clear water in which to live.** 	*7. How many of these reasons would apply to this crocodile?* 

The night-shift

As day changes to night, most animals retire to their nests and burrows. Night-time (or nocturnal) creatures take their places and share their space and food. Instead of hawks there are owls. Instead of butterflies there are moths.

How do animals see in the dark?

Many nocturnal animals have fine hearing, or large eyes that can see very well in the dark.

Owls are one of the few types of bird which hunt at night. Owl eyes are a hundred times sharper than human eyes. Owls can spot a mouse by candle-light 91m (300ft) away. They also have excellent hearing to help them find prey.

8. Owls cannot move their eyes in their heads. True or false?

Bats are such successful hunters that one in four mammals on Earth is a bat. They hunt with their own unique animal radar system.

Bats make high pitched clicking sounds. Their big ears pick up the echoes these clicks make. The echoes tell the bat what the countryside looks like and where its prey can be found.

9. Do vampire bats really exist?

How do bats tell the clicks from the echoes?

So they are not confused by too much sound, bats' ears "switch off" when the click is made. They "switch on" a millisecond later to listen to the echo.

10. Bats can pick up radio signals. True or false ?

How do glow-worms glow?

Glow-worms and fire-flies light up at night. Two chemicals in the tail react together to produce a cold yellow-green light. Despite being so visible they are rarely eaten by predators because they taste horrible.

11. The glow-worm glows to: a) read at night; b) attract a mate; c) light the way for other animals.

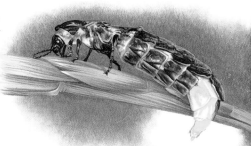

12. Which one of these is not a night-time animal: a) hedgehog; b) mouse; c) eagle; d) potto; e) nightingale?

Why do some animals only come out at night?

Fewer animals are around at night so there is less competition for food. This suits small and timid animals like this African potto.

13. The potto is a type of: a) lion; b) loris; c) lizard.

Most predators hunt during the day. Animals such as this mole, which is almost blind, have less chance of being eaten at night.

14. Where do moles make their homes?

In very hot parts of the world, the heat of the day is tiring. This kangaroo rat comes out at night when it is cooler.

Did you know?

Some frogs and toads do not mind the taste of glow-worms. Sometimes they eat so many they are lit up from inside.

15. In some countries fire-flies are put in lanterns and used for lighting. True or false?

The open ocean

The oceans take up 71% of the world's surface. The Earth's first creatures lived here 3,500 million years ago. Now the oceans are home to a huge variety of animals.

Some areas of the sea are as different from each other as rainforest and desert. Surface winds, light, depth, currents and temperature all affect the amount of life in the sea. This map shows in white which areas of the ocean are the richest in life.

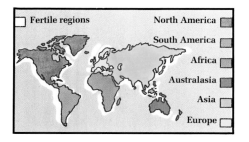

1. What do the most fertile regions of the sea have in common?

2. Which is the biggest ocean?

Who lives in the sea?

Along with fish, animals of almost every type can be found in the sea. On this page are some of the main ones.

Most fish, such as these cod, have bones and shiny scales. The scales overlap and form a flexible, streamlined skin.

3. A group of birds is called a flock. What is a group of fish called?

4. Fish sleep: a) upside down; b) in a glassy-eyed trance; c) lying on the sea bottom with a pebble as a pillow.

Some fish, like the shark, have soft, rubbery skeletons and scales as rough as sandpaper. Fish like these lived in the sea before dinosaurs existed.

Crustaceans like this lobster have hard shells and legs. Shrimps and crabs are also crustaceans.

A few reptiles, like this turtle, live in the sea.

5. Which one of these is a crustacean: a) pangolin; b) piddock; c) prawn; d) pirana?

Some birds, like this cormorant, can dive underwater to hunt for fish.

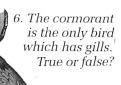

6. The cormorant is the only bird which has gills. True or false?

Mammals like this sea lion, and seals and whales, also live in the sea. They cannot breathe underwater but can hold their breath for a long time.

7. Which of these birds is not a good swimmer: a) penguin; b) petrel; c) puffin; d) parrot?

How do fish breathe underwater?

Fish suck water over rows of feather-like gills, at the back of their mouths.

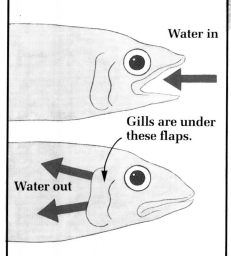

Water in

Gills are under these flaps.

Water out

A fish's gills filter oxygen from the water in a similar way to how our lungs take oxygen from the air.

Why do whales leap?

Some whales occasionally leap out of the water, landing with an immense splash. No one knows for certain why they do it. The following reasons have been suggested:

1. To communicate with other whales. The sound of the splash travels far.

2. To let the whale see further than it can at sea level.

3. To shake off little creatures which live on the whale's skin.

Humpback whale

8. Do you know what this sort of leaping is called?

9. What sort of animals live on whales: a) jellyfish; b) barnacles; c) sharks?

10. When whales give birth, how many calves do they usually have?

What is plankton?

Any sea creature that drifts with the tides and currents instead of swimming, is called plankton. Most plankton are microscopic, but some, like jellyfish, can be quite large. There are two main types of plankton, called phytoplankton and zooplankton.

Phytoplankton are tiny plants. They need light to live, so they are found in the top, sunlit layers of the ocean. They provide food for many different animals.

Zooplankton are animals. They eat each other and phytoplankton. Many are minute crustaceans or newly hatched eggs.

12. Are herring plankton?

Phytoplankton magnified thousands of times.

Zooplankton magnified hundreds of times.

11. A cubic metre (1.3 cubic yards) of seawater can contain 200,000 plankton. True or false?

13. Plankton is a Greek word that means: a) wanderer; b) sea food; c) microscope?

Why do deep sea fish look so extraordinary?

Deeper in the ocean it is very cold and below 600m (1,970ft) it is pitch black. Very little lives here so deep sea fish have to make the most of any chance they get to eat.

Over half the deep sea creatures can light up parts of their body. As well as a lure for prey, these lights are used to attract a mate in the total darkness.

14. What do you think this fish is called: a) a viper fish; b) a gobble fish; c) a fanged blemish?

15. The lights on deep sea fish are solar powered. True or false?

The mouth can be opened very wide by unhinging the bottom jaw. This enables the fish to eat large prey.

Did you know?

Sharks have a row of teeth on a kind of conveyor belt in their bottom jaw. If they bite something tough and their teeth fall out, other teeth move up to replace them.

Luminous spots act as a lure for prey.

Curved, sharp teeth make it difficult for prey to escape.

Life at the edge of the sea

The creatures that live at the edge of the sea are quite different from the animals of the ocean. Instead of open water, they live in mud, rock or coral. For those that live on the shore, the tide comes and goes twice a day, exposing them to both air and water.

Who lives on the beach?

At first glance it is difficult to tell if anything other than seabirds live on the beach. Plants rarely grow here. Only the occasional pattern in the sand gives a clue to the animal life under the surface.

The birds' beaks are various lengths. This lets them search for shells, worms and snails that live at different depths in the sand. They hunt for food right up to the water's edge.

1. Why do you think these birds all have long legs?

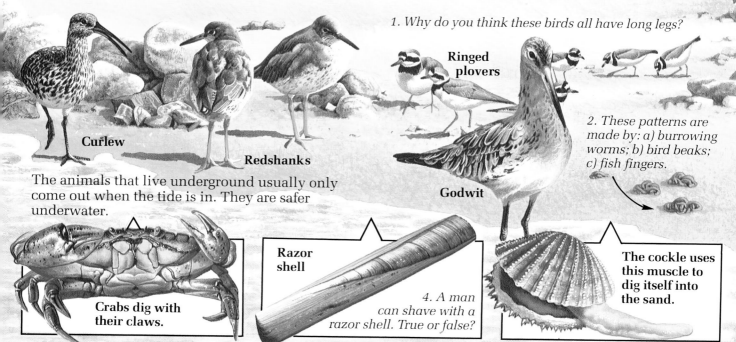

Curlew

Redshanks

Ringed plovers

Godwit

2. These patterns are made by: a) burrowing worms; b) bird beaks; c) fish fingers.

The animals that live underground usually only come out when the tide is in. They are safer underwater.

Crabs dig with their claws.

Razor shell

4. A man can shave with a razor shell. True or false?

The cockle uses this muscle to dig itself into the sand.

3. Which of these causes the tides: a) the moon and the sun; b) the wind; c) earthquakes; d) whales?

5. Which of the animals on this page do people eat?

6. The cockle's digging muscle is called: a) a foot; b) a tongue; c) a toe.

Who lives on the rocks?

Unlike shore animals who can burrow into the wet sand, rock dwellers have to sit out in the open when the tide goes out. They need water in order to breathe, so they will die if they dry out. At low tide, they save a supply of water inside their bodies or shells to prevent this.

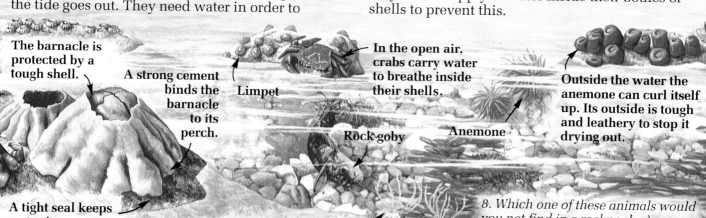

The barnacle is protected by a tough shell.

A strong cement binds the barnacle to its perch.

Limpet

In the open air, crabs carry water to breathe inside their shells.

Rock goby

Anemone

Outside the water the anemone can curl itself up. Its outside is tough and leathery to stop it drying out.

A tight seal keeps water in.

7. Barnacles also settle on the underside of: a) aircraft; b) ships; c) windsurfers.

The barnacle's tentacles wave in the water, picking up food.

Oyster

8. Which one of these animals would you not find in a rockpool: a) sea urchin; b) starfish; c) salamander?

What are coral reefs?

Coral reefs are made up of millions of little animals called coral polyps. Their bodies have hard, bone-like cases and they live together in huge colonies. These reefs are the biggest animal-made structures on Earth. The biggest reef, the Great Barrier Reef, stretches for more than 2,000km (1,260 miles).

Coral reefs are the most colourful and crowded underwater environments on Earth. There is a good supply of food and the reef offers many caves and crevices for shelter.

Where are coral reefs found?

Reefs are found in warm, clear, shallow waters off tropical coastlines and islands. Corals need warmth and sunlight to grow.

9. Are there coral reefs in Europe?

10. The Great Barrier Reef is off the coast of which country?

☐ Coral reefs

North America
South America
Africa
Australasia
Asia
Europe ☐

Great Barrier Reef

Who lives on the reef?

An extraordinary number of different sea creatures live on the coral reef. Most of them are brightly coloured to help blend in with their equally colourful environment. This also helps them recognize their own kind from all the other animals which share their environment.

A triggerfish's hard spine can anchor it into crevices if it is attacked.

Angelfish and butterflyfish have very similar shapes, but angelfish are usually larger.

Cleaner wrasse eat damaged skin off larger fish.

Pufferfish blow up into a ball if threatened.

Corals wave tentacles to catch food.

11. Which other creature on these pages does the coral animal resemble?

Normal size pufferfish

The parrotfish has a beak to crush up coral for food.

12. A parrotfish is called this because: a) it can talk; b) it has a hard beak; c) it lives in the jungle.

Lionfish have poisonous spikes to keep predators away.

Sponge

14. Sponges are used to make sponge cake. True or false?

The stonefish's camouflage makes it almost invisible against the rocks.

Spiny sea urchin

13. What do you think these spikes are for?

Did you know?

When parrotfish go to sleep, they cover themselves with a bubble of slime which they make in their mouths. This stops predators from picking up their scent.

15. The stonefish can kill a diver. True or false?

Living without water

The deserts of the world are wastelands of rock, rubble and sand. Scorching hot by day and bitterly cold by night, they have almost no water.

The largest desert is the Sahara, which stretches from northern Africa into Asia. The map on the right shows where deserts are found.

1. Which of these is not a desert: a) Gobi; b) Kalahari; c) Namib; d)Kenya?

2. Which continent on this map does not have a desert?

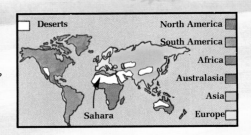

How do animals survive in the desert?

Desert animals cope with sand and lack of water in a variety of ways. The camel is especially well suited to life in the desert.

In the same way that a large pan of water takes longer to boil than a small one, a large animal like the camel stays cooler in the heat than a small one.

Hairy ears and eye lashes, and slit nostrils keep out dust and sand.

3. The hump stores: a) water; b) fat; c) fuel.

An insulating wool coat keeps out both the heat of day and the cold of night.

Animals like this gerbil shelter from the sun in burrows.

Animals like this desert hedgehog come out at night when it is cooler.

Many small mammals have big ears, like this fennec fox. These provide a large surface for heat to escape from, in the same way that soup cools quicker on a plate than in a mug.

Wide feet stop the camel from sinking into the sand.

4. Camels with one hump are called: a) dormitories; b) doubloons; c) dromedaries.

5. A camel can drink 90l (20gal) in one ten-minute drink. True or false?

How do animals move in the desert?

Sand is very tiring to walk on. It can also be scalding hot. Desert animals cope with this in a variety of ways.

The sidewinder snake winds itself along. Only a very small part of its body touches the sand at any one time.

Jerboas take large leaps over the sand.

Where do animals find water?

Rare streams and springs provide drinking water and create fertile areas of plants and trees. Most animals though find their water in food.

6. What are the fertile parts of the desert called?

The Gila monster reptile finds its water from the animals that it eats.

The addax gets all of its water from the plants and grasses in the desert.

7. The addax never needs to drink. True or false?

8. Which is a desert plant: a) daffodil; b) cactus; c) bamboo?

Living at the ends of the Earth

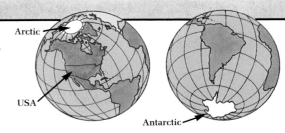

Arctic

USA

Antarctic

The Arctic and the Antarctic are the coldest places on Earth. Very few kinds of animal live here, but those that do can be found in large numbers.

What is the Arctic like?

The most northern part of the world is covered with a great frozen sea – the Arctic Ocean. It is a bleak place. Even in midsummer the temperature rarely rises above 10°C (50°F).

9. What is the central point of the Arctic known as?

Who lives in the Arctic?

The polar bear is the biggest land animal of the Arctic. It is a strong swimmer and hunts seals. The polar bear only lives in this part of the world.

Arctic foxes often follow bears around, eating the food they leave.

Polar bear

Seals leave a breathing hole in the ice.

Fur under the paws gives a good grip on ice and keeps the feet warm.

Did you know?

In severe snow storms, polar bears scoop out shallow hollows in the snow. They sleep in them until the storm is over.

10. Can you name any other type of bear?

Many seabirds come for the summer, when sea food is plentiful.

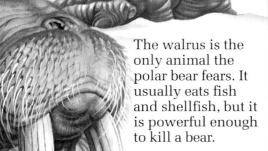

The walrus is the only animal the polar bear fears. It usually eats fish and shellfish, but it is powerful enough to kill a bear.

What is the Antarctic like?

The Antarctic is a huge island, which is one and a half times the size of the USA. Two thirds of Antarctica has been covered with ice for the last four million years.

11. Is the Antarctic bigger than Africa?

Who lives in the Antarctic?

Most animal life is found around the coast, which is the warmest part of the Antarctic. The sea here is full of life and supports vast colonies of penguins and seals. Inland, only a few insects can survive the intense cold.

12. Ninety five per cent of the world's ice is found in the Antarctic. True or false?

Seals live in seas all over the world, but penguins only live on the coasts of countries in the far south.

The Weddell seal can stay underwater for an hour. When it dives, the heart slows down and oxygen only goes to the most vital body organs.

13. Seals are: a) mammals; b) fish; c) reptiles.

The leopard seal hunts penguins.

Are penguins birds?

Penguins are birds that have lost the ability to fly. Instead they have become superb swimmers.

14. Which one of these birds can fly: a) emu; b) kiwi; c) flamingo; d) penguin?

A layer of fat keeps out cold.

Wings act as flippers.

15. Do polar bears eat penguins?

Grassland wildlife

Grasslands (shown in white on the map) are found inland in some hot, dry countries. The countryside is covered in sturdy, long grasses. All the animals shown on these pages, apart from the South American anteater, are found in the vast, open plains of East Africa.

Lions, leopards and cheetahs hunt here, but animals are more likely to die of thirst, hunger or bush fires. They are also in danger from human hunters.

Rhinoceroses, for example, are killed for their horn. Some people believe it has magical powers even though it is made of the same substance as fingernails.

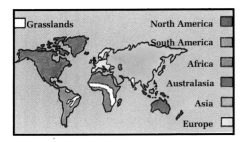

Grasslands | North America
South America
Africa
Australasia
Asia
Europe

1. A rhino uses its horn to: a) burrow underground; b) scratch its back; c) attack its enemies.

2. The horn of a rhinoceros is made from: a) keratin; b) kerosine; c) korma.

Why do so many wild animals live here?

People have not been able to farm this land because it is too hot and dry for farm animals and crops.

There is usually plenty of suitable food for the wild animals that live here, though.

Elephant and giraffe feed on tree leaves.

Wildebeest and zebra graze on the grasses.

The leopard and lion are meat-eaters.

Vultures eat what the hunters leave.

3. Animals that eat plants are called herbivores. What are animals that eat other animals called?

4. How many kinds of animal on this page eat plants?

5. A zebra has black and white stripes because: a) it is a cross between a black horse and a white horse; b) it is camouflage; c) it is blackcurrant and vanilla flavour.

Why do many animals go around in large groups?

Grass-eating animals like the wildebeest and zebra are safest in large groups, or herds. This confuses predators because so many targets make it difficult to decide which one to pick.

Strong animals can shelter weak or very young ones in the herd.

Some animals in the herd can graze while others keep a look out for danger.

Predators such as lions hunt more successfully in groups. They work together to create diversions and ambushes, and share a feast rather than squabble over it.

6. Zebra foals can stand and walk within an hour of being born. True or false?

Herds of up to 10,000 wildebeest travel long distances overland in search of food.

7. Which word is used to describe animals that travel long distances?

8. If lions and tigers mate, their cubs are called tigons or ligers. True or false?

Why do termites build huge mounds?

Termites need a lot of moisture. They cannot survive in the dry heat of the plains so they create a home that suits them better.

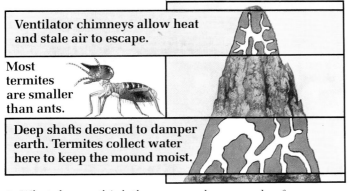

Ventilator chimneys allow heat and stale air to escape.

Most termites are smaller than ants.

Deep shafts descend to damper earth. Termites collect water here to keep the mound moist.

9. What do you think these mounds are made of: a) mushrooms; b) moss; c) mud?

How does an anteater eat?

This South American giant anteater sticks its nose into ants' nests and termite mounds. Its long, sticky tongue shoots out of its mouth at up to 160 times a minute. In this way it can eat up to 30,000 insects a day.

Powerful claws smash a hole in the nest.

10. The giant anteater's greatest enemy is the lion. True or false?

11. An anteater has a large, bushy tail: a) to help it keep warm; b) to sweep its den; c) to hide behind when it is frightened.

Why are elephants and giraffes so big?

An elephant eats twigs, leaves and bark which are difficult to digest. It needs a huge stomach to do this, so its body is big to hold it.

Giraffes' long necks enable them to eat leaves that other sorts of animal cannot reach.

12. Are there any animals in the world which are taller than giraffes?

13. Which one of the animals on this page lives in a termitarium?

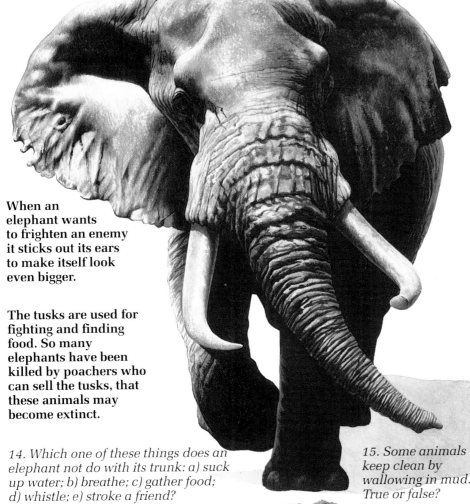

When an elephant wants to frighten an enemy it sticks out its ears to make itself look even bigger.

The tusks are used for fighting and finding food. So many elephants have been killed by poachers who can sell the tusks, that these animals may become extinct.

14. Which one of these things does an elephant not do with its trunk: a) suck up water; b) breathe; c) gather food; d) whistle; e) stroke a friend?

15. Some animals keep clean by wallowing in mud. True or false?

Did you know?

Despite being the heaviest land animals, elephants can move around almost silently. They have soft, elastic pads on their feet that muffle their footsteps.

21

Animal oddities

The shape of an animal's body helps it to survive. It enables it to cope with its environment and compete with other animals for food. The differences between animals help them all fit into their own particular environment.

These two pages look at some of the more unusual looking animals, and how their appearance helps them survive.

Why does the toucan have such a colourful bill?

These colours may help other toucans recognize their own kind among the many brightly coloured birds of the Amazon rainforest.

The bill is useful for reaching into branches for food.

Which animal has eight eyes?

Many spiders have eight eyes but they do not use them all at once. This jumping spider uses different sets of eyes as it stalks prey and then leaps on it.

These eyes detect movement from a distance.

These judge how far away insects are.

These eyes are used when the spider is stalking its prey.

1. Why should you be wary of the red back, funnelweb and black widow spider?

2. Some jumping spiders can leap more than 20 times their own body length. True or false?

Which thorns can move?

These African thorn bugs look like thorns on a branch. When they are still, it is difficult for their enemies to see them. Insects have copied many different shapes to stay hidden from predators.

3. Which one of these shapes is not copied by an insect: a) twig; b) bird dropping; c) red berry; d) snake head?

Why does the luminous jellyfish glow?

This jellyfish drifts in the ocean, coming to the surface at night where it glows softly in the dark water.

Jellyfish move very slowly. They cannot chase after food. The glow attracts prey, and other jellyfish to breed with.

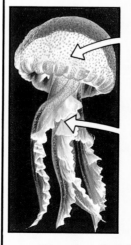

The glow is made by tiny plant-like bacteria, which live in the jellyfish.

The tentacles have stings. They trap prey and discourage animals that may want to eat the jellyfish.

4. What do jellyfish have in common with sea anemones and corals?

5. Which one is not a jellyfish: a) aurelia; b) Portuguese man o' war; c) raspberry; d) purple sail?

Why is the pangolin covered with scales?

The pangolin's body is covered in hard, flat scales made of the same basic substance as your hair and fingernails. If it is attacked it rolls up into an armoured ball.

6. Which other animal in this book has a long sticky tongue and eats ants and termites?

7. Put these animals in order of size: pangolin, jumping spider, platypus, mudskipper.

The pangolin has no teeth. Instead it swallows stones to grind up the ants and termites it eats.

Its long sticky tongue is half the length of its body.

8. South Asian tribesmen make bagpipes out of the hollowed-out bodies of pangolins. True or false?

9. Which is the odd one out: a) rhino horn; b) fingernail; c) pangolin scale; d) elephant tusk?

Why are nudibranchs so colourful?

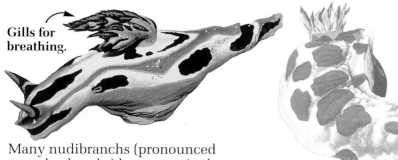

Gills for breathing.

Stinging tentacles.

Many nudibranchs (pronounced new-dee-branks) have amazingly bright colours. This probably warns other sea animals not to eat them as they are poisonous.

10. Which land animal is the nudibranch similar to?

One kind of nudibranch eats jellyfish and corals. It can transfer their stings from its stomach to its own tentacles and use them to defend itself.

What is a platypus?

The Australian platypus is a mammal that lays eggs. It feeds its young on milk (like all mammals) but this oozes out of its skin rather than from the nipples other mammals have.

11. Young platypuses are called platykittens. True or false?

The beak is covered by sensitive skin. It is used to find worms and shrimps in muddy water.

Webbed toes and a flat tail help it swim.

Did you know?

Two platypuses in the Bronx Zoo, New York, ate 25,000 worms a month, along with crayfish, frogs and egg custard. Despite only weighing 1-1.3kg (2-3lb) each, they cost more to feed than the zoo's elephants.

Can a fish survive out of water?

The mudskipper is one of the few fishes that can survive out of water. Like all fish it gets its oxygen from water rather than air. When it comes out of the sea it takes a supply of water along in a chamber inside its body. On land it skips about on muddy shores looking for food.

Which fish shoots insects?

The archer fish of south east Asia shoots drops of water at insects. This knocks them off their perches into the water where they are eaten.

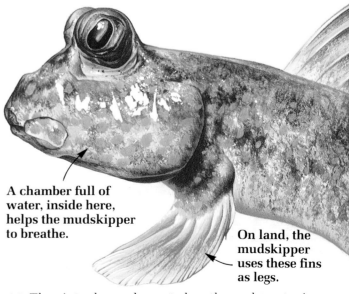

A chamber full of water, inside here, helps the mudskipper to breathe.

On land, the mudskipper uses these fins as legs.

12. Archer fish can also knock birds off their perches. True or false?

13. Would you find the archer fish living in rivers or in oceans?

14. The air tank people use to breathe underwater is called: a) an aqualung; b) an aquarium; c) an aqueduct.

15. Male mudskippers attract females by: a) whistling; b) waving their back fin; c) doing somersaults.

Extraordinary animals

These pages look at animals who are able to do one particular thing better than any other animal.

These special abilities almost always help them find food or escape from being eaten.

Which animal has the strongest bite?

The great white shark almost certainly has the strongest bite. It attacks whales, dolphins, other sharks, and sometimes humans. It is about 8m (26ft) long. The jaw can bite down with a force equivalent to the weight of four elephants per tooth.

1. All sharks are dangerous to humans. True or false?

The shark's teeth point backwards to make it more difficult for prey to escape.

2. A shark's skin is covered with: a) leather; b) barbed scales; c) bone.

3. Which one of these has the shortest life: a) mayfly; b) rabbit; c) goldfish?

Which animal is the most indestructible?

The sponge is a very simple animal that lives in the sea. It eats by filtering food from the seawater that it sucks through its body. If parts of its body are broken off or eaten it can rebuild them. It is so indestructible that if it was broken up in a food mixer it would still be able to put itself back together again.

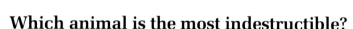

Which is the fastest animal in the world?

The fastest of all animals is the spine-tailed swift. It can fly at 170km/h (106mph).

Swifts spend most of their lives in the air, only landing to have their chicks. They can fly 900km (560 miles) in a single day.

The swift has a very streamlined shape and crescent-shaped wings.

10. Swifts can stay in the air for as long as two years. True or false?

11. What sort of food do you think swifts eat?

The fastest animal in the sea is the sailfish. It can swim at 109km/h (68mph). Its crescent-shaped tail is ideal for pushing it smoothly through the water.

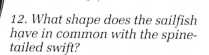

12. What shape does the sailfish have in common with the spine-tailed swift?

Other fast-swimming fish like the tuna and the swordfish also have crescent-shaped tails.

Which is the largest animal that ever lived?

The blue whale is the largest animal that ever lived. It is even bigger than the largest dinosaurs.

It has an average length of 30m (100ft) and weighs 122 tonnes (132 tons). The water supports its huge body.

4. The blue whale sings to other whales when: a) it is having a bath; b) it is happy; c) it wants to let them know where it is.

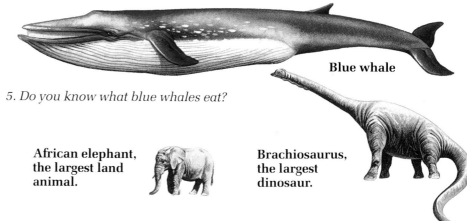

5. Do you know what blue whales eat?

Blue whale

African elephant, the largest land animal.

Brachiosaurus, the largest dinosaur.

Which is the most dangerous animal?

It is thought that mosquitoes have contributed to 50% of all natural human deaths since the beginning of recorded history. They pass on yellow fever and malaria when they feed on human blood.

6. Which of these eats mosquitoes: a) spider; b) snail; c) shark?

7. Which animal on these two pages might you use in your own bathroom?

Which is the greatest traveller?

The Arctic tern makes an annual journey of 38,400km (24,000 miles) from the Arctic to the Antarctic and back. The tern breeds in the Arctic summer. Then it flies far south for the Antarctic summer, which is at the opposite time of the year. It probably does this because the food it eats is plentiful in polar summers.

The Arctic

The Antarctic

8. The Arctic tern experiences more daylight than any other animal. True or false?

9. What sort of food does the Arctic tern travel to eat: a) crustaceans; b) polar bears; c) penguins?

13. Asian princes once trained cheetahs to catch antelope. True or false?

Cheetahs are the fastest land animals. They can run at around 80km/h (50mph) but only for about 400m (440yd). After a short chase they have to stop to cool down and catch their breath.

The cheetah is a medium-sized cat. It is only strong enough to catch small prey, most of which can run very fast. It has to be able to run even faster.

A very flexible backbone gives great power to the cheetah's legs.

Claws act like spikes on running shoes. They give good grip and are especially useful for quick turns.

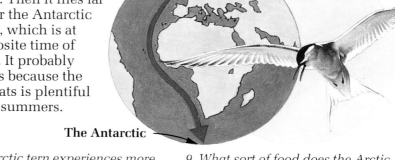

14. Put these cats in order of size: cheetah, domestic cat, lion, lynx.

15. Which of these is the slowest: a) snail; b) sloth; c) stonefish?

Long, light legs take huge strides.

Megaquiz

All these questions are about animals that have appeared in this book. You can write your answers on a piece of paper and then check on page 32 to see how many you got right.

What do you know?

1. In which part of the world did life first appear millions of years ago?
2. Which one of these lived on Earth before the dinosaurs: a) shark; b) sheep; c) squirrel?
3. Which one of these birds swims well under water: a) cuckoo; b) crow; c) cormorant?
4. Which kind of animal can weigh 122 tonnes (132 tons)?
5. What does the cleaner wrasse clean?
6. Can you name one of the two main residents in the sloth's fur?
7. Which are tougher – mice or rats?
8. What makes frogs light up from the inside?
9. How do crocodiles know their eggs have hatched in their mud nest?
10. What makes luminous jellyfish glow?

Silhouettes

These silhouettes are all of animals or objects that are in this book. Can you guess which ones they are?

Which part of the world?

Which part or parts of the world...

1. ...is pitch black all the time?
2. ...are exposed to air and water twice a day?
3. ...is made by animals and stretches for 2,028km (1,260 miles) along the coast?
4. ...shields the lynx from Arctic winds?
5. ...are scorching by day and freezing at night?
6. ...is a frozen ocean?
7. ...have the world's biggest plants and trees?
8. ...are too hot for farm animals but not for antelopes, zebras, termites and anteaters?
9. ...is a whole continent, but inland, only has a few insects living in it?
10. ...have plenty of food and shelter, but also much noise and pollution?

Animal actions

All of these sentences describe a particular kind of animal, or animal behaviour. Can you match them with one of the words from the list below.

1. An animal which hunts other animals.
2. Keeping an egg warm so it will hatch.
3. Animals which drift in the sea.
4. An animal which feeds milk to its young.
5. How animals change to suit their environment over many thousands of years.
6. Sleeping through winter to avoid the cold.
7. Animals which come out at night.
8. An animal which eats plants.
9. An animal which lives on land but returns to the water to breed.
10. A large group of plant-eating animals.

Evolution   Predator   Nocturnal   Herbivore   Amphibian   Herd   Hibernation   Incubation   Plankton   Mammal

Close-ups

These are all parts of animals that have appeared in this book. Which animals are they?

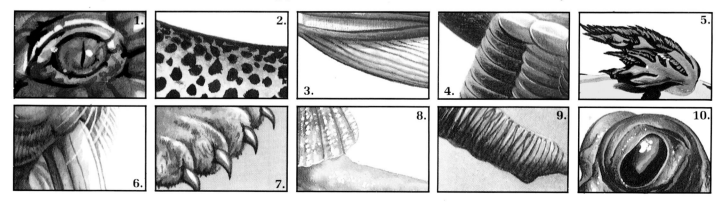

Where in the world?

Can you name these animals and match them with the country, continent or region in which they live?

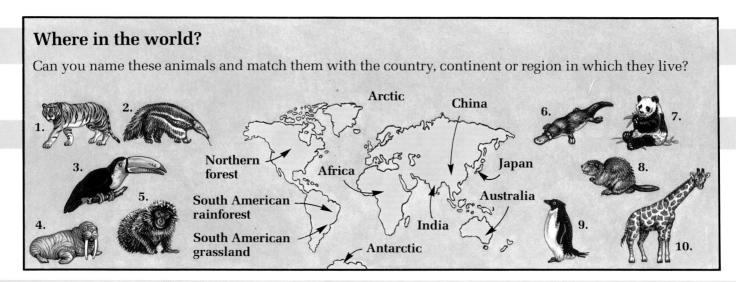

True or false?

1. Lionfish eat zebrafish.
2. Gorillas are vegetarians.
3. Whales cannot breathe underwater.
4. Pigeons have evolved from penguins.
5. Almost three-quarters of the world is covered with water.
6. One in four mammals in the world is a bat.
7. When animals hibernate their blood freezes.
8. Some frogs can fly.
9. The rhino's horn has magical powers.
10. Mudskippers eat mud.

Which animal?

1. Which reptile winds itself along the desert leaving wavy lines in the sand?
2. Which mammal has a tongue half the length of its body?
3. Which insect eats its mate?
4. Which fish sleeps in a bubble of slime?
5. Which mammal's fur grows from its stomach towards its back?
6. Which fish blows itself into a ball if threatened?
7. Which rodents have spread throughout the world on ships?
8. Which bird flies from one end of the world to the other, twice a year?
9. Which insect can eat plastic wiring?
10. Which fish shoots drops of water at insects?

What eats what?

Which of these animals eats the animal or plant in the blue panel below?

Odd one out

1. Which one of these has only one or two babies at a time: rabbit, whale, rat?
2. Which one of these is not a night-time animal: moth, tapir, owl, butterfly?
3. Which one of these is plankton: anglerfish, walrus, jellyfish, lobster?
4. Which one of these cannot survive out of water: mudskipper, crab, anemone, sole?
5. Which one of these northern forest animals does not hibernate: woodchuck, lynx, lemming.
6. Which one of these seashore creatures does not burrow under the sand: cockle, crab, razorshell, barnacle?
7. Which one of these only lives in the Arctic: seal, walrus, Arctic tern?
8. Which one of these animals is not a herd or pack animal: wolf, lion, gorilla, leopard?
9. Which one of these is not a fish: lionfish, butterflyfish, silverfish, pufferfish?
10. Which one of these is a fast mover: army ant, sloth, anemone, tuna?

Quiz answers

The answers to the 12 quizzes from *The animal world* to *Extraordinary animals* are on the next four pages. Give yourself one point for every answer that you get right.

The chart below helps you find out how well you have done in each quiz.

0-5	Read through the answers, then try the quiz again. See how many answers you can remember this time.
6-10	Quite good. Think more carefully about the questions and you might get more answers right.
11-14	Good score. If you get this score on most of the quizzes, you have done very well.
15	Excellent. If you do this well in more than half the quizzes, you are an animal expert!

Your score overall

You can find out your average score over all 12 quizzes like this:

1. Add up your scores on all 12 quizzes.
2. Divide this total by 12. This is your average score. How well did you do?

General knowledge

All the answers to general knowledge questions are marked ★. These questions are probably the hardest in the quizzes. Add up how many of them you got right across all 12 quizzes. There are 40 of them in total. If you got over 25 right, your general knowledge is good.

The animal world

★ 1. Snakes are reptiles.
★ 2. Humans are mammals.
★ 3. The ostrich cannot fly.
★ 4. b) The zebra is only found in Africa.

Zebra

Africa

★ 5. The kangaroo carries its young in a pouch. Baby kangaroos are called joeys.
6. b) Dogs are found all over the world.
7. True. The whale is a mammal.
★ 8. Nine. The seal, lobster, shrimp, crab, octopus, seashell, ray, cod and grouper live in the sea. (Crocodiles are found by river banks and swamps.)
9. c) The salmon is a fish.
10. a) Charles Darwin. He suggested the theory of evolution in his book *On the origin of species* published in 1859.
11. c) The iguana is not an insect. It is a reptile.
12. Lions are carnivores.
13. a) When a whole species of animal dies out, this is called extinction.

The dodo became extinct by 1800.

14. True. The Ancient Egyptians worshipped a cat goddess called Bast.
15. The right order for this food chain is cabbage, caterpillar, thrush, fox.

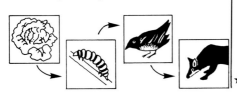

Animal families

1. The correct order is: b) sperm whale; a) elephant; c) giant clam.

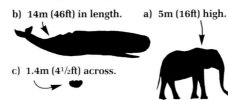
b) **14m (46ft) in length.**   a) **5m (16ft) high.**

c) **1.4m (4½ft) across.**

2. c) Warming an egg to hatch it is called incubation.
★ 3. Penguins eat fish.
4. False. Penguins cannot fly at all, though they are very good swimmers.
★ 5. Ducks' eggs are bigger than hens' eggs.
6. d) A rocket fish is not a real fish.
7. b) Beating the chest is intended to drive away enemies. Gorillas are really quite gentle, and will rarely attack.
8. Gorillas are herbivores. They eat food such as celery, sugar cane, nettles and thistles.
★ 9. Cuckoos lay their eggs in other birds' nests – leaving them with the task of guarding and feeding their chicks.
★ 10. The kangaroo is only found in Australia, as is the koala bear, emu and duck-billed platypus.

Koala   **Emu**

11. b) Crocodile eggs are covered in mud to keep them warm. Mud keeps heat in like a blanket.
12. False. As far as anyone knows, crocodiles cannot be taught to waltz.
13. True. Baby scorpions will eat each other if there is no other food around.
14. a) Honeybees perform a complex dance to tell other bees in their group where to find food.
★ 15. The cells are made of wax.

Staying alive

1. True. This helps tigers to stalk their prey. They can only run fast over short distances so they need to surprise their prey to catch it.
2. a) Tigers like to eat wild pig.
3. Leopards usually hide their prey in a tree where other carnivores cannot reach it.
4. c) A poodle. The wolf is the largest member of the dog family.

     Wolf
Poodle

5. b) Lions hunt in packs.
6. b) Moray eels can grow to be 3m (10ft) long.
7. Angler fish use this lure for bait. It entices other fish, who think the lure is food, within range. Score a point if you got the general idea.
8. True. Most webs only last about a day. They are made of silk, which the spider can eat and use again.
9. True. The chameleon can change its colour to match its environment.
10. True. The sole can match the squares within three or four minutes.
11. True. The sting is shaped like a hook and buries itself into the bee's victim. The bee tears open its tail when it flies off. Although it dies, its action may have saved other bees.
12. b) Many lizards can shed their tails if they are grabbed by them.
★13. Baby spotted deer are called fawns.
14. c) The South American llama is not a deer. It is a relative of the camel.

Llama   **Camel**

★15. Caterpillars turn into butterflies or moths. Score a point if you got either or both answers.

Northern forest animals

1. The northern forests cover land in the continents of Europe, Asia, and North America.
★ 2. Humans have hunted the lynx for its fur.
3. The pine marten is named after the pine tree, which is common in the northern forests.

Pine trees

4. True. The moose is the biggest member of the deer family.

Southern pudu. The smallest member of the deer family.

Moose

★ 5. d) The tree tops are too cold and too exposed to danger to offer a good place to hibernate.
6. b) The thrush migrates. All the other animals live in one part of the world all year round.
7. a) The lemming's greatest enemy is the owl.
8. c) You would find beavers in Canada.

Beaver

Canada   USA

9. True. Both beaver parents build small canals to help ferry logs to build their dams.
10. The lodge is made of the same material as the dam – wood, grass and mud.
11. The underwater entrance makes the lodge especially safe. Any creature wanting to get in would have to be able to swim and dive underwater.
12. False. The bears of the northern forests hibernate in winter.
13. b) These bears are grizzly bears.
14. a) The Moscow State Circus trained two teams of bears to play ice hockey (complete with skates and sticks).

15. True. In the wild, bears also eat fish, small mammals and fruit.

Rainforest animals

1. There are no rainforests in Europe. It is too cold for rainforests.
2. True. The harpy eagle is strong enough to carry off a monkey. It can also carry off a sloth.

Harpy eagle

3. False. As far as we know, sloths do not snore.
4. b) Sloths sleep for 15 to 18 hours a day.
5. c) Jaguars are too heavy for thinner branches. They are clever hunters though and can stalk their prey on the ground and even in water.
6. True. The capybara is the largest rodent in the world.

Capybara

Mouse

7. False. The tapir is a plant eater. It comes out at night because there are fewer animals around that might catch and eat it.
★ 8. Parrots eat fruit and seeds. Score one point for either or both answers.
9. d) The condor is not a parrot. It is a type of South American vulture. There are 315 different types of parrot in the world.

Condor

★10. The marmoset is a monkey, like the howler and spider monkey.
11. True. A marmoset is about the size of a kitten. It is the smallest monkey in the world.

Marmoset   **Kitten**

12. No. If it has to, a sloth can move at 1 km/h (0.6mph), considerably faster than army ants.
13. Yes, rainforests do have people living in them. Pygmies and Amazonian Indians are rainforest dwellers.
14. c) Howler monkeys can be heard 16km (10 miles) away.
15. b) The tapir makes the least noise, to avoid being heard by hunting jaguars.

City wildlife *and* The night-shift

★ 1. In the legend, the Pied Piper drove rats out of the German town of Hamelin. When the town council did not pay him his agreed fee, he took all the town's children and they were never seen again!
2. b) The tile termite is not a real insect.
3. c) A fly usually lives for 10 weeks.
4. False. Mice and rats are both rodents, but they are not the same species.
5. b) A female rat can have 12 babies every eight weeks.
★ 6. Pigeons are seen most in any city. They do not need to hide themselves because they live in places that are difficult to reach.

Pigeon

7. Two. Crocodiles are too big to find shelter, and too dangerous to live close by humans. Score a point if you got either of these answers.
8. True. Owls' eyes are too large to move in their heads. They make up for this by being able to turn their heads around almost half a circle.

1   2   3

★ 9. Yes, vampire bats do exist. They prefer cattle blood to human blood though.

Vampire bat

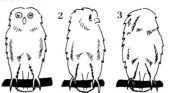

10. False. Bats cannot pick up radio signals.
11. b) Glow-worms glow to attract a mate.
12. c) The eagle is not a night-time animal.
13. b) The potto is a type of loris. Lorises are forest-dwelling mammals, similar to monkeys.
★14. Moles make their homes in the ground. They are small, burrowing mammals which eat worms and insects.

Entrance to burrow

Mole

15. True. The light of several fire-flies is just bright enough to read by.

The open ocean

1. The most fertile areas of the sea are all off the coast. Score a point if you got the general idea. Shallow seas usually have the most life, and water is always shallow by the coast.
★ 2. The Pacific is the biggest ocean in the world. It contains 52% of the world's sea water.

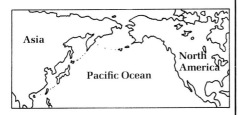

★ 3. Large groups of fish are called shoals or schools. Score a point for either.
4. b) Fish sleep in a trance. They have no eyelids so their eyes stay open when they sleep.
5. c) The prawn is a crustacean.

Prawn

6. False. No birds have gills.
7. d) The parrot is not a good swimmer. Parrots live in trees in rainforests.
★ 8. Whale leaping is called breaching.
9. b) Whales often have barnacles living on them. These are usually found on the head, flippers and tail.

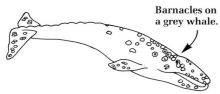

Barnacles on a grey whale.

★ 10. Whales usually have one or two calves. These calves are born at sea. Some sea mammals, like seals and walruses, have their calves on land.
11. True. Plankton are so tiny that 200,000 could live in a cubic metre (1.3 cubic yards) of sea water.
★ 12. Herring are not plankton. They can swim independently of the ocean tides and currents.
13. a) The word plankton comes from the Greek word *planktos* which means wanderer.
14. a) This fish is called a viper fish. It is about 30cm (1ft) long.

The hatchet fish is another type of deep sea fish.

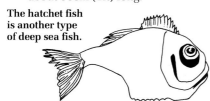

15. False. The light comes from pouches of luminous bacteria on the side of the fish.

Life at the edge of the sea

1. These sea birds have long legs so they can wade in the shallow water at the edge of the beach.
2. a) These patterns are made by burrowing worms.
3. a) Tides are caused by the moon and the sun.
4. False. However, razor shells are called this because they look like old-fashioned razors. This shape helps them move up and down quickly in their burrows.

Old-fashioned razor

★ 5. People eat crabs, oysters and cockles. Score a point if you got two or more of these.
6. a) The digging muscle is called a foot.
7. b) Barnacles settle on ships. In fact they settle on most things in the sea, from driftwood to discarded shoes.
8. c) You would not find a salamander in a rock pool. Salamanders are amphibians which usually live in mountains and caves.
9. There are no coral reefs in Europe. The water is too cold for coral.
★ 10. The Great Barrier Reef is off the coast of Australia.
11. The coral animal looks rather like the sea anemone. They both come from a class of animals called coelenterates (pronounced sel-ent-erates). Their bodies are very similar in structure.

Coral   **Anemone**

12. b) The parrotfish takes its name from its hard, parrot-like beak. The coral that it crushes makes sand for the nearest beach.

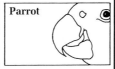

| **Parrot fish** | **Parrot** |

13. The sea-urchin has spikes like sharp knitting needles, to protect it from being eaten. Some fish can bite off the spikes though, leaving it defenceless.
14. False. Sponges are not used to make sponge cake.
15. True. Stonefish have poisonous spines on their backs which can be fatal to any diver that steps on them.

Poisonous spines

Stonefish

Living without water *and* Living at the ends of the Earth

1. d) Kenya is not a desert. It is a country in eastern Africa.

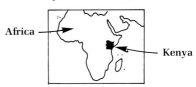

2. Europe is the only continent which does not have a desert.
3. b) The camel's hump stores fat.
4. c) Camels with one hump are called dromedaries. Camels with two humps are called bactrians. You can remember which is which if you think of a D for Dromedary as having one "hump", and a B for Bactrian as having two "humps".

Dromedary

Bactrian

5. True. Camels can drink up to 136l (35gal) in a single day when they get the chance.
★ 6. Fertile areas of the desert are called oases.
7. True. Vegetation can provide all of the addax's water requirements.
8. b) The cactus is a desert plant.
9. The central point of the Arctic is known as the North Pole.
★ 10. Score a point if you got one or more of these: black bear, brown bear, grizzly bear, Himalayan bear, Kodiak bear, sun bear.
11. No, Africa is over twice the size of the Antarctic.

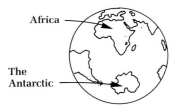

12. True. The Antarctic is almost entirely covered in ice. In some parts this ice is over 3km (2 miles) thick.
13. a) Seals are mammals, like whales and walruses.
14. c) The flamingo can fly.

Flamingo

15. Polar bears probably would eat penguins if they lived in the same part of the world. Fortunately for the penguins who live in the Antarctic, polar bears only live in the Arctic.

Grassland wildlife.

1. c) The rhino uses its horn to attack its enemies.

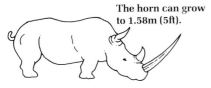

The horn can grow to 1.58m (5ft).

2. a) The horn is made from keratin.
★ 3. Animals that eat other animals are called carnivores (from the Latin *carnis* – flesh, *vorare* – to devour).
4. There are four. The rhino, elephant, zebra and wildebeest are all plant-eaters.
5. b) The stripes are for camouflage. They are especially good at disguising the zebra's shape from a distance.
6. True. New-born zebras are in great danger from predators. Walking with the herd protects them.
★ 7. When animals travel long distances this is called migration. Zebras and antelopes also migrate across the grassland in search of food.
8. This is true, but it only ever happened in zoos, when the two animals were kept together. In the wild, these two animals live in different parts of the world.

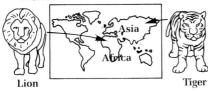

Lion   Tiger

9. c) Termite mounds are made of mud. Termites make the mounds by chewing earth and forming it into mud bricks.
10. False. The lion lives in Africa, and the giant anteater lives in South America.
11. a) The anteater's bushy tail helps it keep warm. It curls its tail around itself when it is cold.
12. No. The giraffe is the tallest animal in the world. Some giraffes grow as tall as 6.1m (20ft).

13. Termites live in a termitarium.
14. d) An elephant does not use its trunk to whistle, though it can make a loud trumpeting noise with it.
15. True. Elephants, rhinos and hippos cover themselves in mud to keep clean. When the mud dries it falls off, taking with it irritating ticks and fleas.

Elephant

Animal oddities

★ 1. All three of these spiders have poison powerful enough to make people ill. Score a point if you guessed they were poisonous.

Black widow spider

2. True. Jumping spiders can jump impressive distances. When they stalk their prey their eyes turn from green to brown.
3. c) Insects copy all these shapes apart from the red berry. Red berries are eaten by birds and are very conspicuous.
★ 4. Anemones, corals and jellyfish all have stinging tentacles.
5. c) The raspberry jellyfish is not a real jellyfish. There is one called a sea wasp though, and another called a sea gooseberry.
★ 6. The giant anteater also has a sticky tongue and eats ants and termites.
★ 7. From the biggest to the smallest, the right order is pangolin, platypus, mudskipper, jumping spider.

Pangolin 90cm (36in).

Platypus 70cm (27in).

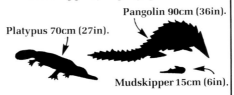

Mudskipper 15cm (6in).

Jumping spider 1.25cm (½in).

8. False. (Pacific islanders use a shell called a conch as a trumpet though.)
9. d) Elephant tusks are made of ivory. Everything else on the list is made of keratin.
10. The nudibranch is similar to a slug.

Slug

Nudibranch

11. False. Platypus babies have no special name. There are usually one or two of them in a litter.
12. False. Birds are too big, both to be knocked off, and eaten.
13. Archer fish live in rivers. There are very few insects in oceans.
14. a) The air tank divers use is called an aqualung.

Aqualung

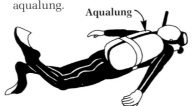

15. b) Male mudskippers attract females by waving their back fins.

Extraordinary animals

1. False. Of 250 types of shark, only 20 are known to eat humans. Most will swim away if they see a human.
2. b) A shark's skin is covered with barbed scales. These cut or bruise any animal that brushes against the shark.
3. a) Mayflies only live for a day as adults. They hatch, lay eggs and die.
4. c) It is thought that whales sing to let other whales know where to find them.
★ 5. Blue whales eat plankton. They have huge brush-like bristles in their mouths, called baleen. These filter the minute plankton out of the water.

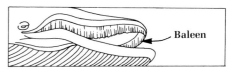

Baleen

6. a) Mosquitoes are eaten by spiders.
★ 7. You may find a sponge in your bathroom. Most bathroom sponges are likely to be artificial ones though.

Artificial sponge   Natural sponge

8. True. Arctic and Antarctic summers have very long days and very short nights. Some terns have lived to be over thirty, and have probably flown a distance similar to the moon and back – over 800,000km (500,000 miles).
9. a) The Arctic tern eats crustaceans.
10. True. Young swifts spend the first two years of their life in the air.
★ 11. Swifts eat insects.
12. The crescent shape. This is ideal for pushing an animal smoothly through air or water.

Swift

Crescent shape

Sailfish

13. True. Cheetahs were used to hunt antelope. They wore hoods until they were unleashed, like trained falcons do today.
★ 14. From largest to smallest the correct order is: lion, cheetah, lynx, domestic cat.

Lion 3.5m (11ft).

Cheetah 1.75m (6½ft).

Lynx 1m (3½ft).

Domestic cat 0.75m (2½ft).

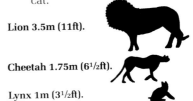

15. a) The snail is the slowest. Garden snails move at 0.05km/h (0.03mph).

Megaquiz answers

There are 100 possible points in the whole Megaquiz. If you score over 50 you have done well. Over 75 is excellent. You can find out more about each answer on the page listed after it.

What do you know?

1. The sea (page 14).
2. a) shark (page 14).
3. c) cormorant (page 14).
4. Blue whale (page 25).
5. Other fish (page 17).
6. Algae, or moths (page 10).
7. Rats (page 12).
8. The glow-worms they have eaten (page 13).
9. The babies squeak (page 5).
10. Luminous bacteria (page 22).

Silhouettes

1. Jellyfish (page 22).
2. Scorpion (page 5).
3. Pufferfish (page 17).
4. Termite (page 21).
5. Flying squirrel (page 11).
6. Shark (page 24).
7. Termite mound (page 21).
8. Rhinoceros (page 20).
9. Turtle (page 14).
10. Bat (page 13).

Which part of the world?

1. The depths of the ocean (page 15).
2. The seashore (page 16).
3. Great Barrier Reef (page 17).
4. The northern forests (page 8).
5. The desert (page 18).
6. The Arctic (page 19).
7. Tropical rainforest (page 10).
8. Grasslands (page 20).
9. Antarctica (page 19).
10. Cities (page 12).

Animal actions

1. Predator (page 6).
2. Incubation (page 4).
3. Plankton (page 15).
4. Mammal (page 2).
5. Evolution (page 3).
6. Hibernation (page 8).
7. Nocturnal (page 13).
8. Herbivore (page 3).
9. Amphibian (page 2).
10. Herd (page 20).

Close-ups

1. Crocodile (page 5).
2. Cheetah (page 25).
3. Blue whale (page 25).
4. Spine-tailed swift (page 24).
5. Nudibranch (page 23).
6. Walrus (page 19).
7. Tiger (page 6).
8. Cockle (page 16).
9. Elephant (page 21).
10. Mudskipper (page 23).

Where in the world?

1. Tiger/India (page 6).
2. Giant anteater/South American grassland (page 21).
3. Toucan/South American rainforest (page 22).
4. Walrus/Arctic (page 19).
5. Macaque monkey/Japan (page 9).
6. Platypus/Australia (page 23).
7. Panda/China (page 12).
8. Beaver/Northern forests (page 9).
9. Penguin/Antarctic (page 19).
10. Giraffe/Africa (page 21).

True or false?

1. False.
2. True (page 4).
3. True (page 14).
4. False.
5. True (page 14).
6. True (page 13).
7. False.
8. True (page 11).
9. False.
10. False.

Which animal?

1. Sidewinder snake (page 18).
2. Pangolin (page 22).
3. Praying mantis (page 5).
4. Parrotfish (page 17).
5. Sloth (page 10).
6. Pufferfish (page 17).
7. *Either* rats *or* mice (page 12).
8. *Either* tern *or* Arctic tern (page 24).
9. Termite (page 12).
10. Archerfish (page 22).

What eats what?

1. (j) Seal (page 19).
2. (d) Zebra (page 20).
3. (i) Greenfly (page 3).
4. (f) Grass (page 20).
5. (h) Tapir (page 8).
6. (b) Mouse (page 13).
7. (a) Coral (page 17).
8. (e) Salmon (page 9).
9. (g) Monkey (page 10).
10. (c) Leaves (page 2).

Odd one out

1. Whale (page 4).
2. Butterfly (page 13).
3. Jellyfish (page 15).
4. Sole (page 7).
5. Lynx (page 8).
6. Barnacle (page 16).
7. Walrus (page 19).
8. Leopard (page 6).
9. Silverfish (page 12).
10. Tuna (page 24).

Index

First published in 1992 by Usborne Publishing Ltd, Usborne House, 83-85 Saffron Hill, London EC1N 8RT, England. Copyright © Usborne Publishing Ltd 1992.

The name Usborne and the device 🐝 are Trade Marks of Usborne Publishing Ltd.

Printed in Hong Kong / China **UE**